About the Author

Vivienne, at seventeen, was a naive young girl who took things at face value that intentions were good, not knowing that behind the smiles she sees some were untrustworthy, then one day it hit home, to take deeper look behind the smiles, a lesson learned that she carried throughout her life. Some would say it's a positive thing she learned early on, but on the down-side how does one function normally when you build a wall around you, conflicted of who to let in? This impacted Vivienne's life "what's hidden behind the smiles".

The Pain We Leave Behind

To

Emma

Happy Birthday

Eva Dell (pen)

Eva Dell

The Pain We Leave Behind

Olympia Publishers
London

www.olympiapublishers.com
OLYMPIA PAPERBACK EDITION

A CIP catalogue record for this title is
available from the British Library.

ISBN: 978-1-80074-550-6

First Published in 2022

Olympia Publishers
Tallis House
2 Tallis Street
London
EC4Y 0AB

Printed in Great Britain

Dedication

I dedicate this book to Granny Zella-Maud. Without her none of this would be possible.

Acknowledgements

Thank you to my husband, Colin, and friends, Claudette and Mike, for encouraging and helping me write this book

PROLOGUE

One could argue that there is a *greater force* that governs our life, with an invisible story that begins the day we entered the world to the day we leave. It cannot be predicted what the chapters of the story are; or how they unfold; nor can we change what is written. The story can only be changed or altered by the originator, a *greater force*. One would say it's a bit like Pavlov's Dogs.

Vivienne believes her invisible story is the framework of her life. At thirtysomething, some females would normally see themselves as married. That thought may have laid heavily on Vivienne's mind, at one point or another, given derogatory remarks she received from a family member who should have been a guardian.

One night, as Vivienne slept, she had a dream, and in the dream, she found herself having a conversation with a man she'd never met before; and they talked about relationships. In the dream, Vivienne asked the man. "*Do you think I will get married*?" The man in the dream smiled at her and told her the two initials of the man she would marry. Awakening from the dream in the morning she thought no more of it. It was just a dream. But a week later something must have happened, as she remembered the dream again; and decided to write down the two initials in her diary. However, in writing down the two initials, Vivienne thought to herself why two initials, and not the full name? She closed her diary and locked it away.

Vivienne believes the physical and psychological abuse she suffered as a child, and again in her teens, and the excitement she felt when she passed the college nursing entrance exam, only to have it swiped away from her, betrayed by the ones she trusted—those were all chapters of her invisible story.

She considered her life with Bob in the early years, the prejudices she faced, her later life with Bob many years later and wondered what the next chapter holds for the both of them. Vivienne also thought of her son, Rick, and how sad his invisible story had been from an early age, and later on in life with drug abuse. She thought had she done enough for him as a child. Would things have been different, had she stayed and looked after him herself? Vivienne also thought about the next chapter of Rick's invisible story; would he relapse or had he truly been cleaned?

But for Vivienne, she could not predict the next chapter of her invisible story, as she knew that she had no control over what is written.

CHAPTER 1

Bob and Vivienne Steel lived in the leafy Surrey suburbs, one of the greenest boroughs in Greater London. It attracted visitors from near and far: ramblers; artists; photographers; cyclists; tourists; wild-life enthusiasts; and many more.

It was a bright Sunday morning and having finished breakfast Bob said, "Viv, dear! I am going to take a shower and get ready before we go to the art exhibition at the Landmark."

"Okay," replied Vivienne.

Vivienne sat at the breakfast bar with her Union Jack mug of warm tea in hand; she spun the seat in the direction of the bi-fold doors, gazing out down the garden beyond the trees, and drifted off into thought. How different life was from when she was a teenager growing up in Leeds. She drifted deeper into thought and remembered how cold the winter days were in Leeds, and how quickly it got dark in the evenings. She wondered whether people still bought their winter boots in August at Leeds market, in readiness for the cold winter months. She recollected in particular one winter day waiting at the bus stop for what seemed like a lifetime, in a mile long queue in the cold as the snow fell. Vivienne was so cold that she could not feel her toes and her fingers were numb. By the time the bus came it was full and it drove by. Eventually another bus came later and she was able to get on. By the time she got home she could not control the tears streaming down her cheeks. Vivienne's mum asked her what was wrong. She said how cold she was, and that she couldn't feel her toes. Her mum replied, "This is England, love."

Those were cold days. Vivienne shivers.

Bob said, "Viv! Are you not ready for the art exhibition? You seem lost in thought; hope you were at a good place!"

"If only," replied Vivienne. "Anyway," she said, "give me half an hour. I'll quickly go and get ready."

In less than half an hour Vivienne was down the stairs and ready to go. They got in the car and drove to the art exhibition at the Landmark. As they arrived, there was a queue of people with tickets in hand waiting to go in, so Bob and Vivienne joined the queue and after a while showed their tickets and went into the exhibition.

There were many paintings and other artwork on display. They were also some unusual pieces displayed. One in particular from a Danish artist had caught Bob's eyes; it was made of wired torso covered with mesh fabric, sealed with cloth glue, one would imagine.

Bob said to Viv, "Where would you put that piece of art?" pointing to the torso.

Vivienne replied, "Maybe in a library or a large hallway." She couldn't be sure.

Most of the afternoon they spent walking from stall to stall admiring various artworks. Bob and Vivienne saw two paintings they liked and could not decide which to buy. They were looking for a painting for their home in France that they were renovating. Having gone around the exhibition a few more times, they were still drawn to the same two paintings and their decision of which one to buy was made for them as one of the paintings they liked had been sold. They negotiated a reasonable price and bought an S. Harling seaside painting.

On the way home they stopped off at their favourite river view restaurant for Sunday lunch in Teddington. Bob and Vivienne had a good table with view of the boats moored on the river. The familiar waiter came with the menu and they ordered a beer for Bob and Vivienne had a ginger beer. They viewed the menu, decided on smoked salmon starter for Vivienne, and a duck liver pâté for Bob followed by seabass and vegetables for Vivienne and lamb-shank and roast potatoes and spring vegetables for Bob. There were many diners, it being Sunday afternoon. Two celebrities were spotted discreetly dining. It wasn't long before the meal arrived and it was lovely, as always. Attentive waiters came along asked if everything was okay and would they like further drinks, before they moved on to serve other diners.

The meal was tasty and filling, so no dessert was had; instead, Vivienne had tea and Bob had coffee. Later they paid and tipped the waiter, and made their way to their car and onwards home. It was a perfect way to end the day, after the Landmark art exhibition.

CHAPTER 2

On reading the morning paper there was an article about compensating the mistreated Windrush migrants. Bob asked Vivienne whether her father was part of the Windrush generation.

Vivienne replied, "From what Dad told me, he was part of the Windrush era, but fortunately for him he did not arrive on the boat, he came over on the BOAC plane."

In the late 1950s and early 60s, The UK government were in need of workers in the transport industry, steel foundries and nursing. They sent invitations to the heads of government in the Caribbean islands, for people to migrate to the UK to be trained and work in these disciplines. The immigration process was slow and Uriah was the first family member to migrate to the UK.

Uriah was the eldest of nine children to Maud Donna and Danny Johnston. Danny was short in height and of slim build. He was a quiet, small-time farmer of few words, but it was once rumoured within the Maud Donna family that there was a dark side to Danny. Maud Donna was adopted as a child and brought to the hills of Westmoreland to live, where she integrated into her new family. She married Danny when she was nineteen, and together they had nine children; six boys, one of the boys was raised by a friend of the Maud Donna family, and three girls. She was the head of the Maud Donna family, in other words, the Donna. She was instrumental in getting things done. It was agreed within the family that Uriah would be the first to travel to the UK, as he was the eldest of nine; he had previously travelled to California, when he was nineteen, as a labourer, and picked oranges. Uriah's name was put forward; accepted by the government; the necessary paperwork completed; and health checks done. Maud Donna was a proud woman but poor; she borrowed money from friends and neighbours within the district, and with family members contributing, they eventually raised enough money to buy a plane ticket for Uriah. He also had some money to spend. Arrangements were made for Uriah to stay with family friends in Yorkshire, and that they would meet him at the airport. Most of the family members went to see him off at Kingston airport. They waved white handkerchiefs, as he boarded the plane. He left behind: his wife, Isabel, and three children, Vivienne, Giselle and Josh. He also left behind his mother, father and eight younger siblings in Jamaica.

On arrival at Bradford airport, it was minus three degrees. He picked up his bags and made his way through customs to the arrivals' lounge, expecting to be greeted by family friends. To his dismay, having checked around the arrivals' lounge, he could find nobody there to meet him. Thinking they may have been delayed he waited a while, only to find the lounge area empty; and he was the only one around. Uriah did not have a phone number; so, he pulled out the piece of paper from his pocket with the address on it, and decided to ask directions.

With the directions he received and being in a strange country at the height of winter, in the dark, bitter cold and thick fog, he soon realised that his journey would not be as straightforward as he anticipated. He had to get a train from Bradford airport to Leeds train station; then a bus from the

Leeds train station to Chapeltown; and walk the remainder of the journey to the address that he had.

Carrying his bags, he headed for the ticket kiosk, bought a train ticket from Bradford airport to Leeds train station, got on the train and started his journey. The train journey was relatively easy as he was told to catch the direct train from Bradford airport to Leeds train station, and he made sure that he double-checked with the train guard before he got on the train. As he disembarked the train in Leeds, he asked directions to the bus terminal, and made his way there, but he noticed that all the buses had numbers on the front in lights. He then asked around what bus it was that went to Chapeltown and was shown by an attendant.

He finally, got on the bus; and asked the conductor if this was the bus to Chapeltown and he said yes.

"Take a seat. I will be around to sell you a ticket."

Uriah then showed the conductor the piece of paper with the address, and asked if he knew where the address was.

The conductor replied, "You're not from around here, are you?"

Uriah replied, "I am from Jamaica."

The conductor replied, "That's a long way away," and continued, "I can drop you off in Chapeltown, but for the address I don't know where that is. I just sell and issue the tickets."

Uriah said, "Thank you very much," found a seat and sat down. Later the conductor went around issuing tickets and collecting fares.

Now seated on the bus, Uriah pulled his bags close to him. He watched as the bus pulled out of the station; he looked around taking in what he could through the thick fog, as the bus moved swiftly along. Then, about ten minutes later, there was a shout from the conductor saying, "Chapeltown." Uriah stood up, unsure, with his hand on his bags. The conductor continued, "Darkie, you get off here.

Uriah looked in amazement and quickly walked to the opened door, said thank you and got off the bus.

He later thought about why the bus driver called him 'Darkie'. Could it be because he didn't know his name? Uriah, new to the country, did not realise it was a derogatory term used to addressed black people.

With the piece of paper in hand and address given to him by Maud Donna, Uriah carried on walking until he found the street. Now all he had to do was find the number of the house, which he did, not long after. Feeling pleased with himself that he was finally at the end of his journey, although he was bitterly cold, he knocked on the door. The family were pleased to see him and invited Uriah in. They apologised to him for not being there to meet him at the airport. They said that they couldn't get the time off work. He was so glad to be out of the cold and into the warm house that he didn't mind.

They talked about the relatives they had left in Jamaica, and how they were doing, as he handed them the gifts of mangoes, breadfruits and yams that his mum had sent for them. They offered him a seat; a hot drink and something to eat. They later showed him around the house and where he would sleep.

Uriah asked after a job, and they told him they would talk about that the following day. It was such a long day for Uriah; he thanked the family for their generosity; said good night and went to bed. He slept as he'd never slept before.

They all had breakfast the following morning. But today for Uriah would be more of a relaxed day, for him to familiarise himself with the surroundings. He was shown around by a family member.

The next day he made his way to the Labour Exchange to register for work. On arrival he found a long queue of migrants waiting to be registered. After several hours of persevering, it was his turn. He then went through the process, was registered; given a National Insurance Number and a card for a job to work in the steel foundries.

CHAPTER 3

Uriah's first day at work was surreal, to say the least, in comparison to that of Jamaica. Everything in the UK was more uniform and a process had to be followed.

The supervisor showed him around as part of a group; they were shown a clocking-in card with their names printed on. The supervisor said, "You need to punch this card before you start work and when you've finished work; it is also an offence to clock in for someone else." He continued. "If you don't clock the card with your name on, you don't get paid on Friday. Is that understood?"

They agreed as a group.

Uriah was a quick learner and could be charming when he needed to be. He was friendly, a Christian, and familiarised himself with his workers, some of whom also were from his island. Once he was settled in the job, some of them would say a short prayer before they started their shift. At lunchtime they often brought their lunches, as they weren't accustomed to the British diet, and they sat around in small groups and ate in the warm foundry with the heat; they being used to the heat. During lunch they often talked about the parishes they were from, or the island they came from, and the families they had left behind. Most of all they looked forward to Friday, their first pay-day, when they would send money by postal-order form to their families.

Six months later, Uriah was promoted and made head of the migrant co-workers. If they were issues between the migrant workers, Uriah would see they were resolved and that those issues did not escalate up the chain.

CHAPTER 4

Maud Donna and the family agreed that Evan, the second son, would be the next to travel to the UK. Evan was a builder by trade and a very good one. He was proficient in the houses he built, be it from timber or brick. Evan filled out the necessary papers; completed the health checks required; and was accepted. It was now a year since Uriah arrived in the UK, and with him being in full time employment he sent money to his mum, Maud Donna, to pay back the money she had borrowed to buy his plane ticket. Having paid off her debts, she saved enough from what Uriah sent her to invest in farm animals and was now in a position to help Evan with his plane ticket and spending money.

Evan's plane ticket was bought and he was on his way to the UK. He would be staying with the same family who received Uriah. Evan had all the instructions from Uriah of how to get to Chapeltown in Leeds. Uriah knew the day to expect Evan and he kept a look out for him, only to see him walking with his suitcase toward him in Chapeltown. Uriah could not believe that his brother had arrived, and he was over the moon to see him. Evan settled in with the same family and shared a room with his brother.

Evan had left behind a wife, in Jamaica, and he hoped that she would join him later, but it was later understood that she had no interest in joining him in the UK. Years went by and she took ill and died from ovarian cancer. Evan did not attend his wife's funeral, for whatever reason. It could be that he could not afford to go, or it could be other personal reasons. Maud Donna took care of his wife's funeral.

Evan was now integrated into the British way of life. He received his National Insurance Number and, with the help of the Labour Exchange, he found a job within his trade. Evan made many friends within the building trade. He was quite knowledgeable within his field and his opinion on building work was valued, even though his wages said otherwise. Evan socialised with his co-workers, and went out for drinks with them.

Evan and Uriah must have been like chalk and cheese when it came to socialising, and they must have made interesting lodgers; one was a Christian who attended church every Sunday, and the other enjoyed a good drink with his mates at the pub. However, one would like to think they respected each other and that they got along. Evan and Uriah found a flat with two rooms and moved away from the family had who received them, but always kept in touch with them nonetheless. They needed a bigger place because Isabel, Uriah's wife, would be joining him in a year or so.

CHAPTER 5

Isabel joined Uriah one year after Evan had arrived. They all shared the two-bedroom flat. Isabel signed on at the Labour Exchange and got her National Insurance Number, and not long after she found a job at Hepworth Clothing. Isabel had previous experience in sewing. She learnt sewing from a seamstress in Jamaica who made exceptional clothes for the whole district. Isabel made friends in her new job, and in conversation, she mentioned that her brother-in-law was sharing with them and that he was unmarried. One of her work colleagues in particular, Hetta, seemed interested, as she was herself single. Isabel discussed it with Evan and Uriah when she got home, and they invited Hetta to dinner one Saturday afternoon to meet Evan.

Hetta was a bright and talkative person which encouraged Evan to come out of his shell, him being an introvert like his dad, Danny. Uriah was sceptical and unsure that they were a good fit. Uriah thought she was too dominant in comparison to Evan's wife who had passed, who was not a loud person. It could be that Uriah was just being protective of his younger brother, as he was dyslexic.

Hetta seemed more knowledgeable about things than Evan, and in conversation they also learnt that Hetta had left seven children back in St Thomas with different fathers. That was a red flag! However, as time went by, Evan and Hetta got closer, and a year later they were married. They found a place of their own where they lived. They had one daughter named Angie, who was a female carbon copy of her dad, Evan.

CHAPTER 6

The next child that Maud Donna planned to send to the UK was Rosa, the youngest child. The Maud Donna family got together to discuss the possibility of Rosa going to the UK as the third to leave. Rosa gave all sorts of excuses as to why she did not want to go to the UK.

The fact was that she had a boyfriend named Rufus; and, also unknown to the family, she was pregnant. Rufus later left her, and went to the UK himself. He promised Rosa that he would send for her, but he didn't. When he arrived to the UK and was settled, he found himself someone new, got married and started a family. Rosa eventually accepted the fact that Rufus had betrayed her.

She later married Ray from the district. He had recently returned from the USA, and she probably thought he had money. Maud Donna met with Ray's family and a wedding was planned for Rosa and Ray, and not long after they were married. They had five children, and others from previous relationships.

At first everything in the marriage was fine, but as the years went, and with her having so many children, their relationship deteriorated. Ray treated her poorly, both physically and psychologically. After having all those children Rosa gained much weight; it was as if she had given up on life and was just going through the motions. Rosa had lost her one true love. She had many regrets with the decisions she'd made, with previous opportunities that were given to her. She often wondered what her life would have been like, had she gone to the UK.

Rosa is today surrounded by some of her children and grandchildren; some have refused to have anything to do with Ray, their dad, given how he mistreated to Rosa. Some of her children live abroad and keep in touch by phone.

After Rosa's refusal to go to the UK, Maud Donna enquired within the family which other family member would like to go travel, be it to another country, not necessarily the UK.

CHAPTER 6

Maud Donna's third son, Alfred, was a successful tailor, and had a tailor shop in Savalamar, Westmoreland. Alfred was married to Isa and they had two children, a boy and a girl. The boy was bright and had passed his common entrance exam, and was accepted into one of Westmoreland's most prestigious schools, Manning's. The marriage between Alfred and Isa did not last long and they were later divorced. The children were seven and nine years old and were sent to live with the Maud Donna's family. The children's mum, Isa, then disappeared and so, the Maud Donna's family blamed her for the breakdown of the marriage. No one really talked about the breakdown of the marriage in details, it was all hush hush.

Maud Donna's family agreed it would be best for Alfred to migrate and he chose to go to Canada. He worked in Canada as a tailor, in his known discipline, and was successful at it. He later took his children to Canada with him. It was told that he often holidayed and visited certain resorts in Jamaica every other year. His life in Canada was fulfilled in some respects and he lived there for many years. It was later learnt that Alfred was gay and hadn't come out. Outsiders of the Maud Donna's family now began to put the pieces of the puzzle together, of his hush hush divorce; and the reason his marriage ended.

Alfred became ill with an AIDS related illness and deteriorated. He spent his remaining life in Canada, and was cared for by his two children, and later died from AIDS. His son brought home his ashes home to be buried in the Maud Donna's family plot. His daughter never returned to Jamaica from the day she left the island as a child.

After Alfred's passing, both the children were reunited with their mother; who filled them in on how she was treated; through no fault of her own. The reason she did not speak out at the time was that being gay was not talked about; it was a taboo subject. Also, given that Alfred was from the large Maud Donna family, she just quietly went away.

After what was revealed, the children are no longer in communication with Maud Donna's family, but they're trying to make up for the years they lost with their mum.

CHAPTER 7

The fourth son of Maud Donna's family was Aston. He had no wish to travel to the UK; his preferred choice was Canada, followed by the USA, and so it was. Aston was married to Jane and they had five children. They also had a successful grocery store that sold most things. Aston first migrated to Canada and worked on the farms picking oranges and lemons. When the season ended, he went back home to work in the grocery store with his wife; they also invested in farm animals. When needed again, his employers sent for him, and that was how it worked. He often bought stock from Canada to sell in the shop his wife, Jane, managed. They would sell ladies' underwear, blouses, shirts and items that could not be found in Jamaica at the time. He had three consecutive farm-work trips to Canada.

Aston later migrated to the USA where he did similar work to that he'd done in Canada, picking oranges; until in he retired to Jamaica in the mid-90s. He helped his wife in the managing of the grocery store. He also had many farm animals that he cared for and often sold livestock at the markets.

Aston was known to be fairly well off in a monetary sense. He worked hard during his young days; and invested his money wisely. The majority of his children excelled, and travelled the world, while the odd one who turned to alcoholism. Aston would often help the under privileged children and would give them lunch money for their school lunch. However, some of the same children he helped grew up to me be monsters.

It was said that Aston had just been back from selling some of his livestock at the market and had a fair amount of money on him. Whilst he was alone in his store, three masked men entered and robbed him of the money. He fought against them but the odds were not in his favour. They cut off the money belt from around his waist and took the money. It was said in the struggle Aston may have recognised one of them; and they cut him in the stomach and left him bleeding to death on the ground with his intestines hanging out. He was taken to hospital but pronounced dead on arrival.

CHAPTER 9

Maud Donna's fifth son was Pierre, who made it known to the Maud Donna family from day one that he had no intentions of travelling to the UK, USA, Canada or elsewhere, if it meant him boarding an airplane. Pierre had a fear of flying and no one could get him on a plane. Pierre was married to a local girl from the district, Doris. They had three children, a boy and two girls, all of whom where reasonably successful; the boy did exceptionally well. He passed his common entrance exam and was accepted into Manning's, a school that had been established for generations. That gave him a grounded foundation. He in turn became a shrewd businessman in his own right.

Pierre and his wife had a successful retail business and were well known and respected within the district and surroundings parishes. Pierre was very vocal and enjoyed a good debate; while Doris was more on the quiet side, but she would come alive when Pierre was having strong a debate.

Later in life, Pierre retired and now enjoys visits from his children and grandchildren and great grandchildren.

Pierre once told a story of a visit he had to the doctor who told him he had cancer and prescribed him treatment for him. Pierre asked the doctor if he would lose his hair. The doctor said yes. Pierre told the doctor he'd rather not take the treatment if he was going to lose his hair, and it was thought that Pierre was vain. He later had a second opinion with a different specialist. When the results came back, he found that his first diagnosis was wrong and that he did not have cancer. Pierre said, always get a second opinion. Pierre had other age-related ailments, but not cancer.

However, one thing still laid heavily on Pierre's mind. Of all the nine children, Maud Donna had, why was he the one she gave away? It is thought that Maud Donna explained to Pierre that the woman was a family friend, who could not have children. Even though Pierre's life was enriched with his adopted parents, he still struggled with how Maud Donna made the decision of which child to give away.

CHAPTER 10

Maud Donna's sixth and youngest son was Ellis. He was a true Jamaican, and was also of the same opinion as his brother, Pierre. He would not leave Jamaica, nor would he travel to any other country, at least not by plane. Ellis was an extrovert and was in his comfort zone when working on his farm and tending to his animals. He was of slim build and could often be seen walking with his machete tucked under his arm or on his hand. Ellis was married to Lynne, a local girl from the district and they had three children, two boys and one girl, who did reasonably well. In later years he had many grandchildren who enriched his life. He was close to his eldest brother, Uriah, and often carried out odd jobs for which Uriah insisted he was paid. They had mutual respect for and valued each other's opinion. As in all large families there were always disagreements but nothing that could not be sorted out.
Whilst working on his farm, Ellis became ill. It is not known exactly what happened but he developed problems with his breathing which deteriorated rapidly. Because Ellis lived alone, he asked Uriah if he could stay with him, and Uriah refused as he preferred his own company and was used to living alone. This led to Ellis moving to Kingston to be looked after by his son. However, Ellis's condition worsened and he died. Uriah struggled in coming to terms with Ellis's death, blaming himself for not helping him in his hour of need, this led to Uriah having a breakdown and then becoming senile.

CHAPTER 11

Hyacinth was the first daughter of Maud Donna. She got pregnant at an early age and was married to George, who was much older than her. They had five children fairly close in age; and it would have been inappropriate for her to travel abroad. In the early years of their marriage her husband treated her poorly; she was often running back to the Maud Donna family home, and then she would return to her husband. He would often hit and cut her, leaving marks that are still visible to this day. However, her children did very well, all of whom travelled, and living abroad. Hyacinth now spends her time travelling between the USA and Jamaica seeing her children and her grandchildren. Later on in life, her husband mellowed and they communicated better; with no abusive behaviour, they also travelled together while they visited their children. Hyacinth was a home maker for her family and her children came first.

Hyacinth once said of all her children, there was one that was exceptional, and that she could put her pot on the fire and know that money would be on its way to buy the goods to fill the pot.

CHAPTER 12

The second daughter of Maud Donna was Dahlia. In her younger days she was the wild one; the life and soul of the party who enjoyed a good dance or sing song. She was short in height like her dad, Danny, and she was an extrovert and spoke her mind as she saw fit. Dahlia was a happy person and she was the only child of Maud Donna not to be married, but she had the largest family with her partner, James. They had beautiful children, a mixture of Indian and Jamaican, with beautiful hair; lovely looking children. She had nine children, all of whom have done very well for themselves. While her children travelled abroad, she looked after the grandchildren. Now that the grandchildren have grown, she lives in Canada with one of her sons and his family. They look after her extremely well and wherever they travel she is always part of the family. Being a closely kit family, they all attended regular family gatherings. She made sacrifices for her children in their younger years; and was always a home maker for them. Now they, in turn, are there for her in every way.

CHAPTER 13

At this point, Uriah and Isabel were making plans to bring the three children they had left in Jamaica—Vivienne, Josh and Giselle—to the UK. They needed a bigger place to accommodate their family, and found an apartment on the first floor with two bedrooms, one of which was in the attic, a large kitchen with dining area, with a sofa that converted into a bed, and bathroom, in an old Victorian house, and moved in. They kept in touch with the family where Uriah first lived when he arrived in the UK. They also had a good network support in the church. A few years later they had their first child to be born in the UK, David.

Vivienne, Josh and Giselle in Jamaica were cared for by family members, until they were in a position to bring them to the UK. In order to achieve this, Uriah and Isabel joined a community 'partner' scheme. This was based on trust and honesty with members contributing a sum of money each week, and at the end of eight weeks it was jointly agreed by the members who received the money. The 'partner' scheme continued until all members had received a pay-out.

Vivienne, Josh and Giselle sat in their seats on the BOAC plane heading for the UK, looking out of the small oval shaped window as family members and others waved handkerchiefs from a platform above the airport terminal.

Vivienne thought to herself how lucky she was to be given the opportunity of living in the UK. As the plane took off from

Kingston airport Jamaica and turned across the sea, it appeared that the plane was below the sea as it climbed a mountain of waves. This seemed strange to her, but this was Vivienne's first time on a plane, and she thought it could have been a mirage.

She remembered how long the journey was and that they stopped twice. The first stop was on a small island to have the plane refuelled and checked over. The second stop was at an airport in New York, for passenger disembarking and others boarding the plane. It was also the first time Vivienne had seen snow. As she looked out of the window of the plane, the snow was thick and appeared like a white blanket covering the tarmac and on the roofs of the buildings.

Whilst in-flight, how annoying it must have been for the passengers as Josh would disturb and ask the time. Josh was eager to get off the plane; he had not been in such a confined space before and was anxious. A male passenger got fed up and said to him, "Why did you come if you didn't want to?"

Having heard that, Giselle began to cry; the journey seemed forever.

The plane touched down at Bradford airport in the night. It was cold and dark, it being January. Dad and his friend met Vivienne, Josh and Giselle as the airhostess handed them over to him. He was glad to see them but made a fuss of Josh; and Vivienne took Giselle's hand and followed behind them to the car. Vivienne thought the journey from Bradford airport to Leeds was long, and that the dark looking buildings were factories, but in fact, she later learnt they were not factories but houses. To her it seemed strange as the houses back in Jamaica were colourful, regardless of whether they were made from timber or bricks.

When they arrived at their new home their mum was glad

to see them, and introduced them to the youngest brother, David, who was two years old at the time. The family spent most of the evening together as they talked about the snow they had seen in New York; the men on the island that refuelled the plane; how annoying Josh was on the plane and how he got told off by the passenger; and how long the journey was. They also talked about the relatives they left back in Jamaica. Both Mum and Dad showed them around the flat, and where they would sleep, and they had dinner as a family.

After dinner, Dad showed Josh how to stack the coal in the fireplace, adding old newspaper before he lit the fire, and how to clear away ashes. Vivienne and Giselle watched.

CHAPTER 14

As time went by, Vivienne, Josh and Giselle tried to adjust to the British climate and culture and how to fit in.

Vivienne did not have any friends and found that life was monotonous. The most exciting thing for her since she arrived was when they all went to C&A to buy winter coats. She chose a dark green coat with accents of plaid at the hem. Giselle chose a red coat and Josh got a thick grey coat. It was the first time they had been on an escalator and they were a little nervous, and Dad told them to hold on tight as it climbed higher.

Vivienne thought that her parents hardly knew her and when they talked it was mainly about how they were treated in Jamaica. Her mum did not tell her about teenage things; what to do and what expect. Vivienne recalled going into the chemist to buy sanitary towels and was so embarrassed to ask for them, that she left without buying any.

Her mum was eighteen when she had Vivienne, and would not have had much experience in parenting, so parenting teenagers would be a strange thing for her. She had been away from her children for so long that she did not know where to begin. She probably did this best she could with what she knew. Uriah had not been around much, him being at work. The siblings who came over were disjointed; like pieces of puzzles, and tried to fit in where they could. Mum's way of communicating was to shout, and Dad's way was to shout, followed by a beating with electrical cable.

Vivienne was invited to enrol in nursing college. The requirement was she had to take a college entrance examination. On the day of the entrance exam, as she entered the room, they were many students, forty students in total. Vivienne was the only black student in the room. She felt strange but she thought they were all students. They all sat and were given sheets with exercises and questions; Vivienne looked at the questions and found them easy, due to the high standard of education in Jamaica from which she left, where excellence was demanded, competitive students and high achievers, in comparison to the British education at the time.

At the end of the exam, the sheets were collected by the administrators, who said, "If your name is called; stand up."

Vivienne's name was the third to be called. Vivienne stood up and one of the administrators looked at her questioningly and said to her, "Are you Vivienne?"

She said, "I am."

The administrator looked puzzled.

Vivienne did not think the administrator was being racist, because she did not know about racism.

Eight of the forty students passed, Vivienne included; and were asked to stay behind to be told what books they had to buy; and the starting date for nursing college. One of the administrators called Vivienne aside and said, "Your parents will need to buy these books. They are very expensive. Can your parents afford them?"

Vivienne said she would ask them.

All excited she went home and told her mum how well she'd done, and her mum was pleased for her. She also told her that the books were a bit expensive. Her mum said she would talk to her dad about them. When her mum asked him, he said that he would not buy the books and Vivienne should go and find work elsewhere. Vivienne was very disappointed.

Vivienne's job now was to look after her youngest brother at the time, David, while her mum and dad went out to work. It was much longer before Vivienne had any friends, and the friends she had were ones from the church or those that lived on her street.

Things got worst and Vivienne at sixteen, suffered physical abused from her dad and ended up in hospital with stitches to her head, because she went to her friend's sixteenth birthday party in the next street without his permission. But for Vivienne, the physical abuse did not start at sixteen, it began way back when she was eight years old. Vivienne recalled it as if it was yesterday.

It was a hot day (*life before the UK*). Vivienne, Josh and Giselle climbed into ackee tree. They shook the ackee tree thinking they would get cool breeze, not knowing the young fruits would fall. Unknown to them, a neighbour was watching them, and reported this to Dad when he got home. Dad was in a fury of rage and grabbed Vivienne by the head, dragged and beat her with the Tobi-switch made from plaited limbs of the tree. He hit her head, and all over her body. He expected her to cry but she defied him and did not cry, and his rage worsened. At this stage Vivienne just wanted to die but still did not shed a tear. The beating was so bad that a family friend, together with Vivienne's mum, intervened. Mum pulled Vivienne from Dad saying, "Are you going to kill her?"

From that day forwarded Vivienne looked at her dad in a different light. She disliked him. Not long after the beating, Mum packed hers and Vivienne's bags and they left for

Spanish Town, to live with Mum's dad. Vivienne remembered how happy she was when they left, everything calm and peaceful. They returned six months later, as the family was divided and Josh and Giselle were missed.

Vivienne often wished her parents were like her friend's parents. As she watched them interacts, they went out as a group, all the siblings and had fun. Vivienne, Josh and Giselle were not allowed out. They often watched their friends go off, leaving them behind.

Living in fear of further physical abuse from her dad, one day whilst he was at work, she packed her things in a black sack and left home. She stayed at a girlfriend's she'd met at church and found a job at Woolworths on the perfume counter.

Vivienne was not streetwise like some teenagers; she wore her heart on her sleeve; took things at face value; and trusted the wrong people. She fell pregnant and had her son, Rick, at nineteen.

She decided to change her life and she left Rick in the care of her mum until she was in a position to take him, moved to London and stayed with a friend for a while in Neasden, North West London.

CHAPTER 15

Whilst in London, she shared room with a friend. Vivienne looked for and found a job. She then found a room to rent and enrolled at the local college in Willesden for further education doing two evenings a week.

She worked for Jon Craig Fashion House in London, in the export department, and was trained by them. The office was large with many desks of electronic typewriters. That was Vivienne's first proper job, and she saw a better life for herself; she was able to pay her rent; and she could send money to her mum for Rick. Her landlady was nice; she went to college two evenings a week; and the people she worked with were nice. In the new job Vivienne made many friends, some of whom were from different Caribbean islands. The accountant was an Indian chap; and the manager was a nice Jewish lady, named Ms G. She said she liked Vivienne's work and thought her typing was neat.

Vivienne was invited out with by the ladies from the office and other staff from the fashion warehouse. They all went to the pub at Friday lunchtime after they got paid, to socialise and get to know one another, with most drinking orange juice, as they all had to work after lunch. As a group they went to the Q Club on Saturday night, where they had fun. They were many guys seen to be interested in Vivienne, but she was on a mission and nothing would get in the way. In her personal life, she found it difficult to let anyone get close to her. She had trust issues and she needed head space. Before she arrived in London, she had felt let down by people she trusted.

The friends she made at that job lasted a long time and one friend in particular had a son the same age as Vivienne's son Rick.

Now she needed to sort out her life, and make it possible to bring Rick to London. Whatever male friends came her way for now would be platonic. Within a year, Vivienne saved as much as she could and found a two-bed flat; she then looked for a school for Rick and brought him from Leeds to live with her in London.

CHAPTER 16

Rick was a happy child but would get anxious if left alone for too long. That stemmed from him being away from Vivienne and she reassured her son that she was going nowhere and that this would always be his home. She would have taken him from her mum before, but in the late seventies and early eighties, she found it difficult to rent a room if there was a child involved. So, she had waited until she was in a position to take him.

He fitted in at school well, but had poor eyesight; and had to wear glasses; he made many friends. Rick was more of a follower, not a leader, which gave Vivienne concerns thinking further along into his education. His friends would often call after school for him to play outside or they would come inside and play table football. He also had a bunk bed so friends could sleep over if they were allowed and it was prearranged with their parents.

When Rick was thirteen years old, he went off the rails in that he wouldn't listened to Vivienne. All he wanted to do was hang out with his friends, and come home at all hours. When Vivienne talked to him, he was disrespectful to her. Vivienne couldn't understand what was happening with him; she then talked to someone who told her it probably had something to do with his hormones. But it got so bad that she decided to move from that area to somewhere new. They moved and his behaviour changed for the better; he later got a pit-bull terrier pup and named it Ruby-jack.

He did well at school and got good grades in languages, but he did not want to go onto college. Vivienne advised him of the benefits of college but he wasn't forced to go. He got a job at a travel agency. Vivienne remembered driving Rick to his first job and picking him up after. However, he did not stay in that job for long, said he found it boring and that there wasn't anyone of his age there.

Rick later found another job at a major airport where people his age worked. He held the airport job for many years and met his girlfriend there; they later moved in together. He went out with the wrong crowd and started drinking and using substances and his relationship with his girlfriend ended and they went their separate ways. He got deeper and deeper into drugs. His dad did nothing; no surprise there. He had abandoned him as a child.

During the crisis of drug abuse, his uncle (Vivienne's youngest brother, Tony), intervened, but to no avail. He was too deep in and as soon as he left Rick's house the drugs people would be back again.

When he couldn't pay the dealers for the drugs, they would cut his wrist, beat him and threaten to kill him; they even smashed in his front door. Rick would often phone his mum asking for money to pay off the drugs people. Vivienne threatened to go to the police but Rick begged her not to, saying it would only make matters even worse for him.

It went from bad to worse and during this turmoil Vivienne thought it was her fault that this has happened to Rick. You see, when Vivienne was pregnant, she'd had the choice of an abortion but couldn't do it, and now she blamed herself for leaving him when he was young. She also blames herself for the turmoil Rick was going through; was this *nature vs nurture*, where a person's behaviour is determined by the environment, either prenatal or during a person's life, or by a person's genes. Vivienne did not know and was confused.

Rick is only alive today because he had a property. Had the drug people killed him, they would have lost whatever money owed them. Or today, Vivienne would be writing a different story about Rick.

Vivienne and her husband, Bob, Rick's stepdad, were there for him. They cleaned up his flat that was in an awful condition; they had to wear gloves as there were used syringes, and other paraphernalia you wouldn't care to mention. His clothes were thrown in piles on the floor in his bedroom and a complete mess. If one could have looked inside Rick's head in those dark days, it would be a replica of the mess in his bedroom.

The garden at back of his flat was a mess with all sorts of on unwanted items, broken bikes, other rubbish, cans. The grass was tall and Bob stumbled on an adder whilst he was clearing up, and was lucky he wasn't bitten. With the whole flat de-cluttered, cleaned and garden cleared, the flat was put on the market and sold and the drugs people paid off.

Rick hired a bodyguard who kept the drugs people away; they knew he was weak plus he had money from the sale of his flat, or what little was left of it.

Vivienne and Bob took him under their wings; he moved in with them; they helped him through the darkest days to put his life back together. It took a very, very long time getting him through rehab and weekly therapy groups. It was a nightmare and one of the lowest points in Vivienne's life. When she had doubts as to whether he was going to make it and doubted herself; Bob was always there saying, "It will take time, we just have to be here for him."

Finally, he turned a corner. He met someone on the Internet, and introduced her to them. Vivienne was sceptical at the time and wondered if he was ready for a new relationship, Vivienne and Bob supported him. It would soon to be Rick's birthday and he had not long passed his driving test. Vivienne gave him a card with a car key inside. He couldn't believe he was given a car for his birthday. He thanked his mum and stepdad for the generous gift.

Rick soon registered at Kingston University, where he studied aerodynamics, nautical engineering. Three years later Rick graduated with MSc Hons (2:1) degree.

Rick now has his own place a few miles from his mum and stepdad. And they hope and pray that he never relapses.

CHAPTER 17

"Viv!" Bob said. "Guess who I saw at the train station, today."

She looked at him, waiting for him to say who.

"Rick," he said. "He seems to be doing well, his chirpy self as usual. Said his car was playing up and that he may bring it round for me to take a look at it."

"Oh! That's good," Vivienne said. "If I know when he is coming, I can make him dinner. I talked to him on the phone two days ago, but he didn't mention it."

Bob was of Scottish origin with blue eyes and blond hair. Vivienne was of Jamaican parents; her mother was mixed race and of light-skinned completion and her dad Jamaican. Vivienne's complexion was more like her mum's, but not as light as her. She was five foot seven inches, of slim build, with long thin legs and arms, straight face, with brown eyes, and a lovely smile when she smiled, and hair below her shoulders.

Vivienne remembered oh so well, the first time Bob introduced her to his family. She met his mum and dad, sister, his niece and two other family friends. They all sat waiting in living room. Bob and Vivienne entered the room and he introduced Vivienne to the family. They both sat down and small talk was made.

Not long after, Bob excused himself and went to the bathroom. After he left the room, the conversation changed and someone blurted out, "I like black pudding."

Vivienne thought, where has that come from, but said

nothing. After the statement was made, there was silence and glances were exchanged, as if, waiting for a reaction. But they were disappointed; Vivienne said nothing.

This was the first time Vivienne felt racism 'up close and personal'. Had this racist abuse happened at her home she would have reacted differently. On the way home in the car Vivienne told Bob what was said when he left the room. He apologised, and said his dad had a strange sense of humour.

Bob and Vivienne were again invited, this time to dinner, and the same group were there. But for Vivienne, it was all about second chances.

With everyone seated to dinner, conversation started and Bob mentioned that Vivienne did not eat meat. Vivienne added, "Vegetables are fine for me."

The male family friend, turned to Bob and said, "Where did you get her from? A Christmas cracker!" He was referring to Vivienne.

Bob did not respond.

Silence fell.

Vivienne thought to herself, another disrespectful remark made towards her by another male in the group; on her second time meeting with them. But she said nothing. Vivienne knew within herself that this was the last time she'd dining with these people.

Would there be a third time? Hell, no!

Later, when Vivienne arrived home, she expressed her feelings to Bob. She told him that she could have done with his support in that situation and was surprised when he'd said nothing, and that she would not put herself in a position for derogatory or racist abuse from his family or their friends again. She told Bob that she didn't have a problem with him socialising with these people, but count her out.

Bob said, "If you don't go, then I won't either."

But she encouraged him to go without her and eventually he went.

One Saturday evening, Bob and Vivienne met up for theatre and dinner. After the meal, as Bob walked Vivienne to her car, a woman handed him a banana and asked him for five pence towards her bus fare. Bob handed her the five pence and told her to keep the banana. However, she did not get on the bus but kept on walking. Vivienne was unaware of what happened until Bob told her a week later. Sometimes it is better not to react to racist's behaviour or remarks as sometimes it can be construed that the person receiving the racist abuse has 'a chip on their shoulder' instead of the narcissistic personality and racist abuser.

Bob and Vivienne on a Caribbean holiday; as Bob read his book in the garden a young lad shouted "hey mister" give me 100 dollars. *Bob thought the boy was being racist as he was the only white person in the garden;* others may think it not racist, but a young boy asking a tourist for 100 dollars. However, Vivienne told the boy not to be disrespectful.

CHAPTER 18

Bob and Vivienne had many holidays within the UK and abroad. Vivienne's parents had a holiday home in Jamaica. They often met up with extended relatives every two years at the family home, in the cool hills of Westmoreland, Jamaica; located between Montego Bay and Negril. It was a place they would go to unwind and get away from it all. More often than not a good time was had, depending on the personalities that were there. However, the downside of being there was that the electricity and water could be cut off at any time without warning. Fortunately, there was a generator at the house that compensated for the lack of electricity and, also a huge water tank with back-up water.

When Bob and Vivienne were in the UK, they arranged for an all-year round gardener, Ziggy, to cut the grass monthly, keeping it low; to prune bougainvillea and shoe-black shrubs. He also looked after the many fruit trees; mango, orange, nectarine, pawpaw, jack-fruit, breadfruit, banana.

They had Kan-I in charge of maintenance, and had been using them for many years. The property was surrounded by painted white walls with a tall iron gate also painted white at the front.

When they visited, Bob and Vivienne would often shop at the seaside market town of Savanna la Mar, which was quite a busy town with street traders in their faces with goods for them to buy, not to mention opportunist pick-pockets edging in closer, as can be found in many busy market towns.

When driving in Jamaica, they found the drivers undisciplined, in that, they only knew one speed—fast—and down the middle of the road. The country roads were narrow and winding, with deep corners, large pot-holes, and steep rock cliff precipices.

But the cool hills of Westmoreland offer benefits; the night sky is often filled with stars that twinkle and sparkle; and often a shooting star goes by, exiting the sky with a long tail, and again re-enters and disappear.

Bob and Vivienne often sat on the veranda and read; and could see the rain, white in colour, coming from the hills towards them and could almost time when it would reach them. Yes, up there in the hills you could observe a lot.

As they sat on the veranda one evening, it suddenly got very cold; you would almost think you were back in the UK. Everyone rushed and put on their jackets. An hour later it was reported on the news about the terrible earthquake in Cuba, where hundreds of lives were lost, not to mention the devastation to Cuba.

When things got overly quiet in the hills, Vivienne and Bob would get in their car and make their way to the holiday resort of Negril.

CHAPTER 19

Vivienne and Bob were introduced by a mutual friend of theirs at a dinner party. When they met, Bob was still living with his parents and Vivienne had a flat; they would often spend weekends at Vivienne's place. He was shy but intelligent and mostly came alive through his witty jokes. Bob was very much sport orientated and played rugby most weekends; he also enjoyed a good plate of food. From what Vivienne gathered of Bob, it would appear that he had not had many relationships before Vivienne. Their sexual relationship was different from any that Vivienne had known; with Bob it was more of a learning curve, but he was a decent and honest man with a good heart; respectful and kind to Vivienne. Bob had all the qualities she wanted in a man and for her, sex, was not the be all or end all, and in time their sex life was good.

They took time getting to know each other and later Bob moved in with Vivienne. They both had busy jobs and at weekends Vivienne would go his games and watch him play.

Bob an avid rugby player and took his games quite seriously. He often trained midweek and played most weekends during the season. Having played rugby from a young age, it is fair to say he was proficient at his game and often coached the colts. After each game you would find him at the club house where he socialised with his team-mates. Vivienne often dropped him off at the games, and then picked him up afterwards.

Vivienne worked as a research executive within drug regulation for a well-known pharmaceutical company, who seconded her to university. She worked there for many years until she retired. She was a keen rambler and often went on walks twice weekly. Vivienne, also a keen keep-fit individual, would work-out two or three times a week at the local sports club. She was also a keen amateur photographer. Vivienne supported many charities: Help the Children Stay in School; Save the Children; Children in Need and Blessings Have to Flow. She supported the less fortunate and deprived children.

CHAPTER 20

Two years after Bob and Vivienne met, they got married on a beach in the Seychelles, in the Indian Ocean, on the island of Mahé and then went onto La Digue.

Oh yes! The two initials Vivienne was given by the man in her dream did match her husband's name.

It was just the two of them, the minister and the two witnesses. The only worry for Vivienne was that her dress arrived on time as it was on the next boat to the island; and that, it wouldn't rain.

On the day of the wedding, Vivienne looked up at the sky, it being crystal blue and the sun shining brightly, with no rain on the day. The gods smiled on them. It was truly a magical day. Their wedding day made the local paper of the island. They later had a church blessing and reception in Jamaica for extended family members.

Twenty-seven years later Bob and Vivienne are still together and have been married for twenty-five years.

They love and respect each other; they have disagreements like any other married couple, but they work through them. Passion may not be as it was twenty-seven years ago, but at the end of the day, they are there for each other; they are soulmates and best friends.

Vivienne loved surprising Bob. He worked hard and she felt it was good to give him a treat now and then. He often spent a great deal of time working on the house when he was not at the rugby games. They would often have days out in London to dinner and theatre. One of Vivienne's surprises for Bob's birthday was a visit to the Shard, with champagne and ice-cream, followed by an afternoon tea, at Harrods tea room. Another one was surprise cocktails at Vertigo 42, in London.

One wouldn't say Bob was overly spontaneous, but he was passionate and generous in his gifts to Vivienne. Over the twenty-seven years of being together he had always given her gifts on anniversaries, birthdays, Valentine's Day and Christmas. Vivienne favourite perfumes were Coco Chanel, and Chanel No5, and he often bought them for her.

Bob and Vivienne often dined out at least once a month, sometimes at a quaint Italian restaurant in Kew where the food was delicious, and a lovely restaurant with beautiful art deco interior in Richmond.

Being members of the National Trust, they often went on day trips to Blenheim Palace, Osterley Park and Ham House.

A visit to Richmond Park was by far a favourite of theirs for local walks. They often visited Isabella Plantation and Still Pond, in the summer, and Vivienne took some stunning pictures of the flowers in bloom. Then they would stop off for lunch at Pembroke Lodge.

CHAPTER 21

Vivienne enjoyed her monthly catch-up with her friend, Amber. They had been friends for many years, and both grew up in Leeds, leaving for London at different times in their lives and never looking back.

Amber's husband, Tony, and Bob were friends, and had been for many years, and the four of them would sometimes go out for meals, and drinks at the local pub in Richmond

Vivienne and Amber normally met up at their favourite French café, where they had lunch and put the world to rights. Vivienne recalled telling Amber about the last guy she dated before she got married: Vivienne had an old maroon Volvo car that was always breaking down. Once it broke down in the middle of the Greenford roundabout, but to keep a long story short…

It was one Saturday morning and the car would not start. Vivienne had the hood up and looked to see if she could see what was wrong; she checked the oil and water but both were fine. Then this tall slim chap with the bluest eyes you ever saw came over and asked, "What's wrong?"

Vivienne replied, "Nothing's wrong with me, it's my car."

He looked at her, smiled and shook his head; his piercing blue eyes went straight to the soul. He then fiddled with something near the engine, and it started. She thanked him.

"Owe you one," she said.

He said, "You're welcome. By the way, I am Tomas."

She replied, “Vivienne.” She had seen him before but he was always with a guy and Vivienne thought he might be gay.

Then there was a barbecue and he invited her, and they got talking. Vivienne asked where was his girlfriend and he replied, “Don’t have one.”

She then said, “A boyfriend!”

He smiled and replied that he didn’t bat that way. “Enough about me,” he said. “What about you? Is there a man in your life?”

Vivienne said, “Not at the moment.”

Tomas asked why.

Vivienne said she didn’t have the time for relationships at the moment. Later they met up again and he invited her out, and they went for a meal and then drinks after. When they reached outside her home, they kissed; it was passionate. Vivienne thought he was a good kisser that stirred all kinds of emotions within her. They went out again on a Sunday afternoon for lunch, followed by a drive to a countryside pub, and kissed again. By now both wanted sex. They drove home in his BMW and went to Vivienne’s place and had sex. It wasn’t rushed but steady, hot and steamy. The best sex ever! Never ever, had she had sex like that before; they cuddled and they kissed again. He didn’t leave until the following morning. Tomas aimed to please and did; and they repeated the last night’s performance in the morning again. During the time they dated they spent most weekends together, with the same electrifying sex afterwards. Tomas and Vivienne’s relationship was more of pleasure thing, which suited them; they were both free agents. They often went out, had fun and then more great, hot sex.

Although Vivienne enjoyed what she had with Tomas, she

knew it would not end in the happy ever after; at the point in both hers and Tomas' lives they wanted different things. Had she not met Bob and moved away and left the past in the past, who knows, Vivienne and Tomas might still have been friends, but with benefits. Her friend, Amber, could not stop laughing when she told her.

After lunch, Vivienne and Amber did retail therapy, shopping at the mall, and then, having exhausted the day shopping, they stopped off somewhere for cups of earl grey tea, before making their way to the train or bus station. Then it would be hugs and *bon voyage* until the next time.

CHAPTER 22

Josh was the second child from Jamaica and it took him longer to adjust to this new way of life; he was used to living in a less restrict environment and Dad's parenting could be construed as unorthodox in comparison to today's parenting. The only thing normal to Josh was that he was fed, clothed and kept clean. No television was allowed in the house; as a child he would often sit on the step of the stairs and peep through the cracked door-frame of the neighbour downstairs, and watch *Top of the Pops* on Friday evenings. When the neighbour caught him watching, she filled in the cracks. There were no family times as before in Jamaica, where all the family gathered around and telling stories some of which may not be true. It was good to listen to stories from days gone by, from the older folks.

Instead, now Josh was shouted at, told he was rubbish, and that the only two children worth worrying about were David and Tony, born in the UK. Dad's quick-fix discipline would be to beat him with electrical cable when he did something wrong. When Josh refused to be beaten with electric cable and stood his ground he was sent to a boys' home when he was fifteen years old. Whilst in the boys' home he was sexually abused; this was not mentioned to anyone until he left the home aged sixteen. Vivienne asked him why he'd said nothing when she visited. (Vivienne was the only one who visited him). He said the men who abused him threatened to kill him if he told anyone.

Two months later, after returning home, Josh moved away from Leeds to London with friends. Josh was a friendly young man, more of an attention seeker; he once told a friend he had a red Saab, and he couldn't drive. But he had many friends and was also popular with the ladies. In London he shared with his friends until he met his girlfriend, Nora, in a nightclub. She was Irish and had been living in London for some time. They decided to hook-up and shared a flat in Islington; at the time it wasn't known for sure what Nora did for a living, but it was later revealed that she worked as a care assistant. Josh worked as a car mechanic with very frequent visits to the betting shop.

About six months later Nora fell pregnant, and later had Caroline. Their relationship was not good; he was often abusive to Nora. Josh was fond of the horses and could often be found in the betting shop. He was often lucky with bets and on occasions won large sums of money but, as the saying goes a compulsive gambler never truly wins. He often went to Ascot with friends from the betting world; and spent hours in the pub.

Eighteen months after having Caroline, Nora fell pregnant again with a second child, Chantel, born later. Their relationship became volatile and Josh continued to gamble and drink and his health deteriorated in that he had liver problems. He became bloated, did not eat, and had the shakes. He was a pitiful sight to see at times. He was in and out of rehab and hospital but he just couldn't kick the habit; Nora also drank and that did not help his situation, but that was the kind of lifestyle they led.

Eighteen months after having Chantel, Nora fell pregnant again and had Jade, her third child. Josh went in and out of hospital for treatment and the last time he went into hospital he never came out. He died, aged fifty, from cirrhosis of the liver, three leaving young children under the age of under the age of five.

Vivienne, Giselle and Tony helped raised the children after Josh passed. It was understood that when the girls were at college, Nora changed job to a care assistant.

CHAPTER 23

Caroline was Nora's first child; cared for by Vivienne the first year of her life.

She was of a cheerful personality and enjoyed travelling and had been to many countries, sometimes with friends from her university days. A bright young lady with a sponge-like brain; she did well at the Catholic school she went to; and in college; and onto university where she excelled with a (1:1) MSc Hons degree in marketing and advertising.

Caroline worked as a tester for a well-known banking group, and bought a flat in South London where she lived with her partner.

It's fair to say Caroline did fantastically well, given her early life background.

CHAPTER 24

Chantel, was Nora's second child.

A more serious and quiet personality, she also excelled at the Catholic school she attended and in college. She went onto university and did business studies with a (1:1) MSc Hons degree. She normally planned ahead and was quite level-headed.

She enjoyed socialising and travelling and was a member at her local gym. She worked as an international buyer for H Knightsbridge.

Chantel and Caroline together bought an investment flat which they let. Chantel married and bought a family house with her husband in North London.

It's fair to say Chantel did excellently, given her early life background.

CHAPTER 25

Jade, being the third child of Nora and Josh of mixed Jamaican and Irish parentage, was gifted with a beautiful olive complexion. She had an abundance of beautiful tresses of loose curls hanging down her back and was tall and slim. She travelled all over America doing hair adverts. Of all the three sisters, Jade was the only one that held a British driving licence.

At school, Jade did not learn as quickly as her two sisters. This was soon realised by Chantel who mentored her, with help from Caroline.

Jade also went to a Catholic school and got the grades she wanted for college; then onto university. She studied English literature and she earned (2:1) MSc Hons degree.

She worked as an estate agent and was awarded estate agent of the year at her firm. She had a flat in West London and enjoyed travelling the world over with friends.

It's fair to say Jade did well given the early life background.

CHAPTER 26

Giselle was the youngest child from Jamaica to come to the UK. She was dyslexic and Vivienne helped her with her reading. Vivienne often protected her when she got into scrapes with cousins in Jamaica (although sometimes she also got into scrapes with Vivienne). Giselle was the only sibling in the family that was not physically abused her by dad; but then again, she was the youngest to leave home. She said at one point she saw enough of what he was capable of and it would never happen to her, and she left home early. But she was by far the favourite of her mum, maybe because she was dyslexic.

Giselle had manipulative ways of getting around things to get what she wanted; she often wore Vivienne's clothes without her permission, leaving the smell of perspiration in the armpit. Vivienne's friend, Grace, who lived opposite, was always on the look-out and would tell her. "Viv," Grace would say, "you know your red top? Guess who I saw in it the other day!" She would then hiss through her teeth in disgust, "Only your Giselle.". And that was why most of the arguments occurred with Giselle and Vivienne.

Giselle was self-absorbed and nothing came before her; it was as if the world revolved around her. In her teenage years she yearned for the finer things of life and money to her was very important.

It was no surprise later when in her twenties she moved from Leeds to London. Giselle realised from an early age that, being dyslexic, an office job or one in the stock exchange was a *no*. Therefore, she chose the nightclubs *per se*. Where champagne flowed abundantly with chocolates; and rich men with more money than sense gave great tips, having a fetish for tall, slim, brown skinned and ebony looking, cosmopolitan women, at a beckoning call.

She had a dog of a boyfriend called Freddie who treated her awfully; he controlled her, and took her money, and she wasn't allowed to talk to anyone. Giselle was scared to talk to Vivienne when she visited, in case she said the wrong thing and then got used as a punched bag later.

Vivienne sat Giselle down and talked to her; told that she couldn't carry on like this, crazy Freddie would kill her. Giselle saved up her money until she had the deposit and bought a flat near Queens Park; she changed her job, but was in the same industry, and changed the areas she used to hang out. Her true and trusted friends knew how to reach her. A year later, Giselle heard through the grapevine later that crazy Freddie got into a fight in a club and killed someone, he went to prison for it, and died in prison.

A few years later Giselle met Mike, a bi-racial guy, who had an identical twin brother; his father was African and his mother white. Mike was a lovely chap and all the family loved him; he was good to Giselle. Mike tried to make it into the music industry; he wrote several songs and performed with well-known artists; but he just could not get a record deal.

Then there was a phone call from Mum to Vivienne and she said that she had just received a brown envelope from Mike with a picture of him, and a covering note for her to give Giselle the picture when he'd gone. Vivienne quickly put the phone down and called Giselle and reiterated what mum had told her. Giselle said, “I can’t reach him,” as she cried.

Two days later his twin came and told Giselle that Mike had committed suicide in his car in the park and was found by the police. Giselle was devastated and spent most of her grieving time at Vivienne’s place.

Giselle may not have been physically abused by her dad like her siblings, but she had a lot of sorrow in her life.

Giselle was always immaculately dressed; she spared no expense on herself. And why should she, she had no children. She learned quickly about living in London; and being dyslexic did not stop her from being shrewd in managing her money. With all that said, who am I to sit here in judgement; where people choose to work; you just have to figure out what works for you and what doesn’t.

Many ladies worked in the *nightclubs per se* and have had enriched lives; each to their own, I say!

Giselle now lives in West London with her Italian partner and has been living there for many years.

CHAPTER 27

David was Vivienne's second brother, and the first to be born in the UK. He was twelve years younger than Giselle. David was a sickly child, born with a heart defect; a hole in his heart. His childhood was not a normal one; due to his illness he couldn't do the things other children his age did. He was often short of breath, and his lips turned blue when he attempted to exercise. David attended a specialist school as he could not keep up with mainstream school. He had hospital check-ups twice monthly. As David got older his symptoms worsened and he begged Dad to be taken to London to see if specialists there might be able to help. But Dad told him that God would make him better. David said, "Daddy, I don't want to die, please take me to London." But he refused to take him, telling him it was all in the hands of God, then had David baptised at their church. The control Dad had over Mum must have been so great that she did not intervene.

David would often visit his friends a few doors away, he would slowly climb over the stone wall as he wasn't strong enough to jump it, and hang out with his mates where they played video games.

One evening Dad went home and asked after David. He was told he was playing video games with his friends. Dad went to the friend's house, knocked on the door and dragged poor David out of the house; he pulled him across the gritty stone wall. By the time they reached home his little legs were bleeding with cuts and bruises.

After that, David surrounded himself with pet snakes, and pigeons, and was forced to go to church. After many years of being ill, being in and out of hospital, his organs shut down. David died in the hospital from heart failure and pneumonia when he was eighteen years old.

CHAPTER 28

Tony was Vivienne's youngest brother; second to be born in the UK. He was born one year after Vivienne, Josh and Giselle arrived in the UK. Vivienne remembered visiting her mum and the baby in the hospital; the baby looked strong and healthy. Mum breastfed Tony until he was two years old, as he refused to take the bottle. Growing up, though, he lacked discipline and was spoilt by Mum. Should Mum tell him to go to the shops for her, he would tell her to go herself, and she found that funny. But you couldn't help but like him; he was witty, bright and had a sponge-like brain and an infectious smile.

Vivienne remembered once on a visit to Leeds, Tony was outside, as two girls walked by and he tried to get their attention but they weren't having it. He called at them and said, "BT said it's good to talk," and both girls turned around, laughing. He went down and talked to them.

Tony was a bright child and excelled at all he did. He was competitive and often made sure he was the first to finish his school work correctly, then wondered why he had to sit and wait for the others to finish. He did not realise that each child worked at a different speed. He got bored from waiting and twiddling his thumbs; and later getting into trouble.

The teachers often called Mum and Dad, and talked about the issues they had his with his disruption in class; they said he could be anything he wanted to be; that he was bright and gifted; and he was always the best at what he did. So why wasn't he challenged? He was a young bright black boy in the late seventies in West Yorkshire, where the majority of the pupils were white; and there were no black role models at the time to see his potential in him, and mentor him. He was also excellent at swimming and had many trophies. With no mentorship he went off the rails and dropped out of school and picked up bad influences. He often got into trouble and his parents would be called to come and pick him up from the police station. On one occasion Dad punched him in his mouth at the police station, and knocked out his tooth, blood draining down his clothes. The police warned Dad that if that ever happened again that he would be arrested.

Tony would sit beside Dad and observe him drive, his brain absorbing in everything, unknown to Dad; later when Dad was asleep, Tony took the car and drove it around with his friends, brought it back during the night and parked it. Dad had only realised one morning when he found the car parked in a different place to where he left it.

Vivienne thought if she had stayed longer at home things might have turned out differently for Tony. She may have been able to help him with his schoolwork and challenge him. But in hindsight, staying at home, would have meant putting her life at risk.

In the mid-eighties, Tony, phoned Vivienne and asked her if he could come and live with her and her son, Rick. She said yes. Tony left Leeds for London and Vivienne picked him up at Kings-cross station. He lived with them for some time, then he found a girlfriend, and two years later got married at Marylebone register office. But he was divorced a few years later.

Tony now has two jobs: fitness trainer in a local gym; and, bouncer at a nightclub in the west end of London. He now lives in Kensington.

CHAPTER 29

The years went by of Evan (Uriah's brother), living in the UK. It is not known if he had ever had a holiday within or outside of the UK; he certainly did not return on a holiday to Jamaica. He worked very hard in the building trade and in years earned very good money as a builder. He later developed kidney problems and was in and out of hospital with treatments. Uriah was concerned when Evan went to visit him and had a conversation about his finances, as he knew he was dyslexic. Evan told Uriah that Hetta had sent all their savings to a bank in Jamaica, and that she talked about going to Canada to live. All of Uriah's fears in the early stages were now realised. In no time at all Hetta packed her bags when Evan was on dialysis at the hospital and left, and that was the last he saw or heard from her. Evan's daughter, Angie, was in the army and was not aware of what was happening. Uriah was now the only one Evan had; he was encouraged to live with Uriah and Isabel now they were on their own, but he refused; and Uriah made it a duty to check on him every day. He would phone first thing in the morning and last thing at night.

One morning Uriah phoned Evan and there was no reply, so he jumped in his car and went to his house. He had a spare key so he used it when there was no reply to the door. Uriah walked in calling his name, but there was no answer, so he went into the shower room and was devastated at what he found. Evan had died at some point during the night or morning in the shower. Uriah was truly broken, and blamed himself, that he should have insisted on him coming to live with them. The authorities were notified and the necessary done. The Maud Donna family in Jamaica were notified of what had happened and what Hetta had done. She emptied the bank accounts, and Uriah had to take charge of everything. His daughter was notified, and no doubt she would have let her mum know.

It was not known what happened after; whether the Maud Donna family avenged their son's death. But one year later it was revealed that Hetta took sick and died in Canada.

It is once said the sins of the fathers are visited upon the children; in other words, the children suffer for the bad things done by the parents.

CHAPTER 30

Both parents (Isabel and Uriah) retired and planned to return to Jamaica their country of birth. If truth be known Vivienne and Giselle, thought that it was their dad was the one pushing for Jamaica; and that Mum went along for a peaceful life. As he often said, "England is not my home." The house in Leeds was sold and their belongings went off in the shipping container as returning residents. They had previously built a house in Jamaica on land they had bought many years ago and the house almost ready to be moved in.

When they returned Mum found it hard to adjust to the way of life. In the UK she was used to just hopping on the bus in Leeds where everything was familiar; and meeting up with her friends; coffee mornings. All that had changed.

Mum found the climate very humid. The Jamaica they had left as young people was not the same; she was never relaxed when she went shopping; and there were many pickpockets about. Vivienne encouraged Mum to come for holidays as often as she wanted. "Let me know," said Vivienne, "when you want to come; and I'll book the ticket; and pick you up at the airport." And that's what they did. She was often with Vivienne, Giselle and Tony when she visited; but her base was at Vivienne's.

On a visit to Mum and Dad after they had retired, one morning they all had breakfast as a family. Mum had finished her breakfast and left the table. Giselle, Vivienne and Dad remained at the table. Dad said to Giselle, "So when are you getting married?"

Giselle replied, "Marriage is over-rated!" She then got up, walked away and went outside to smoke.

Then dad said to Vivienne, "When are you getting married?"

Vivienne replied, "Not anytime soon."

Dad obviously did not like any of the answers he received; so he went in for the jugular with Vivienne and told her, "You are damaged goods anyway, nobody wants you."

Vivienne, now feeling like a wounded bird, got up and left the table and told Giselle what had happened. Giselle repeated it to Mum. Instead of Mum pulling up Dad on his outrageous behaviour; her reply to Giselle was, "Maybe he's dying to eat wedding cake."

Giselle, hearing that, hit the roof, and said, "We did not pay thousands of pounds and fly thousands of miles to come here to be disrespected." With that, Vivienne and Giselle packed their bags and went off to Negril resort and only returned just before they left for the UK.

Many years later Mum began to lose weight and it was thought it was due to the hot climate, but on a check-up with the doctors and hospital it was diagnosed that she had cancer of the thorax. She had many treatments of radiotherapy that did not work, and she later passed away from aggressive cancer of the thorax aged seventy-eight.

Those who attended the funeral from the UK were Vivienne, Giselle, Caroline and Bishop Curry. From the USA were bishops and elders known to the family for many years; from Canada were extended families. The majority of the people who attended were also from their district and surrounding parishes. Mum's funeral was a two-day celebration of her life. Her body is laid in the family estate.

CHAPTER 31

Dad was now living alone in this huge house. He adapted to Jamaica's way of life easily, and would drive himself around the island until he began having accidents and his licence was revoked. He then employed a driver to drive him to where he wanted to go, which was mainly to the bank; post office; and on occasions into Montego Bay for hospital check-ups. He was respected. "He left Jamaica as a young man, made good and returned." Everyone looked up to him in admiration, more so the church members. He often visited several churches on Sundays to worship; and as an elder of churches his donations would be substantial. It was also said he had a lady friend from one of the churches he attended.

As the years went by, Vivienne and Giselle did as much as they could for him; he only had to ask for something and it would be on the way to him. Everyone in the district knew him, he had many friends. He had a gardener to cut the grass, a painter for the maintenance of the property and a helper who worked twice weekly. Dad had nothing much to worry about. He had many siblings, most of whom had travelled and retired to Jamaica, and lived not far from him.

Throughout their frequent conversations, Vivienne realised that he was getting lonely; he would often say I am here all alone. She invited him for holidays but he always declined it, saying his travelling days were over. His health was declining, now he was in his nineties. These conversations went on for a long time; he talked about his cataract operation, and the pain in his legs. He talked about the money he had in is accounts and asked Vivienne, Giselle and Anthony to come over so he could add their names on his accounts in case anything should happen to him. Vivienne and Giselle went and signed the necessary documents at the bank. On Vivienne's return to the UK, they heard that Dad's youngest brother had passed; he had not been ill for very long, which was an added devastation to Dad. As he was the eldest, he that thought he would have passed before his youngest brother.

Soon after his youngest brother passed, Dad went rapidly downhill. He became very forgetful and it wasn't safe for him to be left on his own. Vivienne, Giselle and granddaughter, Caroline, went to visit on several occasions. When it became necessary, he went into a private care facility for his safety and for health reasons; he saw a private doctor once a week whilst in care. He often had many visits to the hospital. If money was the way to keep Dad alive, he would be alive today; he had the best treatment money could buy.

At ninety-two his body had had enough and shut down. Dad died aged ninety-two at Savanna la Mar hospital from pneumonia and heart failure on the 6th November 2019. There was a three-day celebration of Dad's life, starting off with a candle light vigil from the church to his home; then the wake. and the feast on the day of the funeral. His body was escorted by the Jamaican constabulary police to the church, and the church was decorated in colours of blue and yellow. Dad's body remains were buried beside his wife on their estate.

CHAPTER 32

Vivienne being the eldest, of the three remaining children, was in charge of sorting out the estate in Jamaica, with the help of husband, Bob, ensuring that taxes, maintenance and utilities bills were paid, until a decision had made between Vivienne, Giselle and Tony about what to do with the property.

Bob, in particular, was very useful, having been an accountant for over forty years and having kept up-to-date with the changes in laws, be it in Jamaica or elsewhere.

CHAPTER 33

Bob as a child at school loved numbers and found them easy to work with, and often helped his friends who struggled with numbers. It was no surprise when he studied accountancy at university, and chose a career in accountancy.

"Last workday today," Vivienne said to Bob, as he readied himself for work.

"Oh yes," Bob replied. "Seems like a lifetime, but a good one, if you know what I mean! I made many friends; and would like to think that my work there was valued.

"That's the attitude," said Vivienne. "You have a good day now!" She gave him a kiss on the cheek and he was off.

Bob worked for the same accountancy firm for forty years. He made many friends; going to work for him was like going from home to home, with things being so familiar after such a long period of working at the same firm. Today would be his last day at work as he was retiring. This gave him mixed feelings; he was happy that he no longer would he be doing the long train journey to work. He would miss the friendships built over forty years; and the social interactions with colleagues, who often asked his advice, with him being knowledgeable with the procedures and processes of the firm.

Unknown to Bob a big retirement party was planned for him. Sitting quietly in his corner office, he packed up his belongings, cleared out the desk drawers and ensured the office was left in a clean, habitable condition for his replacement. He thought when leaving he would just pop in and say goodbye to his mate, Matt.

But before long there was a knock on his office door. It was the directors' executive PA telling him he was wanted in the boardroom.

As he entered the room, to his surprise it was filled with his work colleagues and friends who began singing: "For he's a jolly good fellow, for he's a jolly good fellow and so say all of us."

"Oh my!" Bob said. "This, I didn't expect!"

Tears welled in his eyes, as his mate, Matt, put an arm across his shoulder and said, "All right, Bob?"

He replied, "Oh yes." He thanked everyone for taking time out of their busy schedule for him, and for their support over the years doing number crunching and having a few laughs. He expressed how much he would miss the socialising and recreational visits to the Fox and Duck.

The staff had made a collection and presented him with a signed leaving card, along with a beautiful, engraved, crystal beer tankard and gold watch.

"Thank you all so very much. I will treasure these," said Bob, holding the tankard and gold watch above his head and continued, "How thoughtful you all are. I look forward to reading all the comments in the card. I hope you can all join me in the pub afterwards for a farewell drink. I think the second round is on Matt."

Everyone laughed, as he cut the cake.

Afterwards they all met up in the pub where they had a celebratory drink. Having said all his goodbyes, Bob made his way to the train station to catch the eight-fifteen p.m. train, which was on time, so he climbed in found a window seat, sat and read the newspaper.

As the train arrived at each station, Bob made a quick glance, checking how many stops to go, before he could catch the bus for his final leg of the journey home. Having arrived at his final stop Bob got off the train and he made his way out of the station, and then walked to the bus stop in front of the station.

Soon after reaching the bus stop the bus arrived. He jumped on, showed his bus pass to the driver and headed to his normal window seat where he sat and read his leaving card. This part of his journey normally took about half an hour on a good day. But today the journey seemed quicker; he had a laugh at some of the comments in the card.

When he arrived home, he was met by his wife, Vivienne. She asked him, how was it today? She knew it would not have been easy for him leaving after forty years of service, as many connections and friendships were made, so saying goodbye must have been difficult.

Bob said, "It was okay," to Vivienne, and began telling her about the surprise presentation they gave him; showed her the leaving card filled with signatures; the crystal beer tankard and the beautiful gold watch. "Then we all met up and went to the pub for a drink or two."

"That's lovely," Vivienne said. "It just goes to show how much they valued and appreciated you."

"Ah yes!" said Bob. "But what happens now that I have all this time on my hands?"

Vivienne replied, "Don't forget we have that trip to Italy booked in three weeks. That is something to look forward to! The excursion starts in Rome. That reminds me," she continued, "we must go shopping for some linen shorts and tee-shirts. I heard it can be humid in Rome, in December." Then she continued, "We will just figure it out. For now, just try to relax and take it easy," as she handed him a mug of tea. She thought to herself, I must remember to cancel the alarm set for six-thirty a.m.

CHAPTER 34

On the day of their trip to Italy they drove to the airport; left the car in the long-stay carpark; checked in their bags and had breakfast after. Once they were through customs, they headed to the duty-free shops where they browsed before going to their departure gate. The flight into Naples took approximately three hours, and they were met by the tour bus guide at the airport to travel on to Rome.

Bob and Vivienne thought their tour of Italy was by far the most interesting in comparison to similar trips taken elsewhere. They had a seven-day tour coach trip around Italy. The coach trip was well organised but at times tiring as schedules had to be kept.

From Naples they went by coach to Rome and visited the Colosseum, the Trevi Fountain, Tivoli Gardens, the Spanish Steps, the Vatican and the statue of Saint John Paul II, Saint Paul's Basilica. On leaving Rome, the coach stopped for a while to view the remains of Monte Cassino, the Second World War battle site. They visited the catacombs of early Romans' burial sites, where the Christians worshiped safely as they could not do so openly. Bob went down into the catacombs. Vivienne found them claustrophobic the deeper they went, and she could not continue the journey down.

They also visited Pompeii and saw the mummified remains left behind after the volcanic eruption of Vesuvius. They also climbed Vesuvius, the still active volcano.

A day spent in Sorrento was quite fruitful; a busy market town where traders sold beautiful leather goods.

Bob and Vivienne took a boat trip to the beautiful island of Capri where they stayed overnight as they explored the island. Bob told Vivienne of a strange encounter he had at the hotel whilst she was asleep of strange flying objects in the room surrounding Vivienne during the night. Vivienne asked Bob what were the objects, he told her they were dressed like Romans, said he chased them away! She found it quite strange as Bob is a logical person, but she just smiled. The island was more a celebrity hide-out, with the location of where a Bond film was made, and pretty boutique shops and quaint restaurants.

They had the option of a visit to the Amalfi Coast but declined; as the sheer mountainous sea level drop and small winding roads could not be entertained.

All in all, what they had seen of Italy was good and cultured, and they promised they would return again. On leaving it was a good flight from Naples into London, and having landed and gone through customs they picked up the car from the carpark and went home to familiar surroundings.

CHAPTER 35

Bob and Vivienne, now retired, planned to spend time doing things they didn't do before. They made a bucket list of places to visit:

Taj Mahal, India: Is described as 'a teardrop on the cheek of eternity' and the embodiment of all things pure, and regarded as one of the finest illustrations of Mughal architecture in India.

Niagara Falls, Canada: Taking a cruise on the *Hornblower* and experiencing the falls close up on the Niagara River would be a terrific experience for Bob and Vivienne

Table Mountain, South Africa: They looked forward to seeing the flat Table Mountain that towers over the city like a watchful giant, as described by some.

Great Wall of China: The longest wall in the world, Bob and Vivienne may not be up to the walk of 21,196.18km kilometres, but have been told to expect an inspiring experience of architecture and winding path over rugged country and steep mountains with great scenery.

But their hopes of travel were shattered, due to the lockdown, caused by a global virus that affected many countries; and caused many to be lives lost.

Restrictions were put in place by governments until a cure could be found to keep the virus under control: face-masks had to be worn in public places covering mouths and noses; hands washed regularly and sanitised.

When shopping, a safe distance of two metres had to be kept between individuals; a limited number of items were allowed to be purchased from supermarkets, with non-essential shops closed. Exercising was done in small groups, keeping the two metre distances. These precautions were put in place to stop the spread of the virus until a vaccine was found. It was a difficult time for the world as a whole.

The NHS staff worked tirelessly to help the sick and vulnerable, and in doing so, put themselves at risk.

As Bob flicked through the newspaper, catching up on the latest news, Vivienne scrolled up and down on her smartphone doing the same, finding the latest updates.

They exchanged ideas and talked about the latest new updates on the virus and how it had brought 'the new normal' way of living.

Now having realised that the virus would be around for a long time, Bob and Vivienne made suggestions of activities they could do for their mental health wellbeing:

Vivienne suggested walks along the River Thames into Kingston and/or Richmond.

Bob suggested walks to the train station to pick up the free *Evening Standard* and *Metro*.

Bob suggested they could learn Sudoku, keeping their brains active.

Vivienne suggested they could practice French and become more fluent for when the lockdown restrictions are over

Vivienne suggested a visit to Kew Gardens. "I hear the grounds are still open to the public! Although we will need to book before we go."

Bob said there was a lot of garden work to be done and

the garden fence was in need of repair.

Vivienne said, “We could do some more work on the front porch.”

Settled, they both agreed.

But Vivienne had promised to make Bob a Jamaican breakfast for some time, and since they were in lockdown, what better time to do it. She decided as it took so long to do, she would do the prep when Bob went to bed, then make it in the morning.

CHAPTER 36

The Jamaican breakfast consisted of: ackee and salt-fish, fried bammy and fried dumplings. It was a nice surprise for Bob and he enjoyed the breakfast so much that he had seconds, and so did Vivienne. The leftovers could be put in the freezer when cooled.

After breakfast, Bob stepped out and into the back garden. It being spring he noticed how blue the sky was, with the sun shining brightly. Bob thought to himself, it's a good day to do some gardening work.

He said, "Viv, dear, it's such a lovely morning, I am heading out to the garden to do a bit of clearing up and get rid of those long weeds, disguised as plants."

"Okay, dear," Vivienne replied.

Bob hurriedly pulled on his wellingtons, put on his straw hat and his garden gloves and headed for the garden shed where he kept his tools. He picked up his trowel, fork, rake and wheelbarrow.

He first cleared the dead leaves. Thinking out loud, he said to himself, "It's a shame they aren't many birds around. They would love the bugs from underneath the leaves."

With all the leaves cleared and put into a pile, he then pulled out the long weeds and put them also into another pile. Bob meticulously raked the fallen apples into another pile also; then put it all into the wheelbarrow and onto the compost heap.

He had been working for a few hours when Vivienne

called out through the open kitchen window, "Hello, Bob! Would you like a cup of tea?"

"Love one," he replied.

With the tea made, Vivienne walked steadily down the garden path carrying a tray with two cups of tea and some ginger biscuits. She placed the tray on the garden bench, and they both sat and enjoyed the tea and biscuits and talked about the garden work.

With tea drank and biscuits eaten, picking up the tray, Vivienne made her way back into the house, saying, "You do not need to do everything today, you know what manual work does to your arthritis joints. Besides, Rome wasn't built in a day."

Bob listened curiously and she went back inside.

Bob further did some pruning of the shrubs, cut off the dead wood from the rose bushes, all of which went on the compost heap. He then called it a day for gardening work and cleaned the garden tools, putting them away with the rake and wheelbarrow, and locked the shed door.

With the garden work finished he went inside, pulled off his wellington boots and garden gloves and put them in the utility room and cleaned up for dinner.

After dinner, Bob and Vivienne decided to go for a walk. They put on their walking boots, hats and coats and headed for a walk along the River Thames and into Richmond.

As they reached the riverbank, they realised that the tide was in, so they changed direction and went across the fields, then to the station to get the evening paper. On the way back they decided to catch the bus home to avoid the muddy fields.

It was not long before they were on their way home. As they boarded the bus, they noticed they were the only ones on it, and a few stops along one other person got on and that was it.

Vivienne said to Bob, "It's not looking very good. The roads are empty and the buses too."

Bob said, "That is true, I guess people are being cautious and only go out when it is necessary".

Vivienne said, "Dear God!"

In comparison, the journey took half the time it would normally take. When they reached home, Vivienne made a pizza, which they ate with a glass of red wine.

Vivienne suggested tomorrow might be a good day to practice some sudoku; with that Bob got excited as he would be teaching Vivienne; and it was all about numbers, just up his street. Even better, it gave him a break from gardening.

CHAPTER 37

Bob explained the basic principle of sudoku to Vivienne:

"Fill the whole grid with the numbers one to nine, so that each row and column, and three by three block, contains the numbers one to nine. No numbers in the columns and rows vertical or horizontal are repeated."

Using the Metro as an example; Bob said, "We have easy, moderate and challenging." He continued, "Let us start off with the easy and see which numbers work."

Under his watchful eyes, Vivienne figured out the basic principle. Bob was quite meticulous, him being an accountant, and before long she had the hang of sudoku. She would never be as good as Bob, but she now knew how it worked.

"Anyway," said Bob, "how are you getting on with the sudoku?"

"Got the hang of it!" Viv replied. "Getting there!"

While doing sudoku, Bob mentioned to Vivienne there weren't many birds in the garden in the days he was out there, and nothing of his favourite bird, the robin.

Vivienne said she read somewhere that the breeding time for the robin was in the summer around July/August, when the female sits on the eggs and the male busies itself gathering food. It would appear summer is a busy time for robins.

CHAPTER 38

Another day of garden work, thought Bob, as he stepped out in his wellington boots with garden gloves to hand and his straw hat on his head. He went to the garden shed and picked his tools as he usually did.

A never-ending job, he thought, it being a large plot. Bob carried on from where he'd left off the previous day; but to be honest he'd rather be crunching numbers instead. Some flowers were in bloom that gave a perfumed scent throughout the garden that lifted his spirit.

He quickly sorted out new suckers and seeds, and planted them in areas that looked bare; and replaced with new bulbs the ones the squirrels had dug out.

It would be a short stint in the garden today, thought Bob. He and Vivienne were to visit the grounds of Kew Gardens, which were still open to the public during lockdown, something he'd been looking forward to for a while.

With all the planting done and the tools packed away, he closed the shed door; and headed towards the kitchen. Once inside Bob went to the utility room, took off his gloves, wellingtons and hat, and washed his hands, and Vivienne gave him a mug of tea. After that he went upstairs for a shower and got ready. Vivienne, already dressed, prepared lunch for them to take for the day out.

With Bob and Vivienne now ready, they put their bags in the car. As Vivienne was about to start the car. Bob said, "Tickets!"

Vivienne said, "Checked!" and off they went.

On arrival, Vivienne parked the car in Kew and they made their way to the garden gates. It made a refreshing change not to see a long queue. They showed their tickets and started to take in the ambience.

They walked around the grounds and admired the lovely plants and manicured grounds. They kept the two metres distance between themselves and other visitors; one of the many rules in lockdown, to stop the spread of the virus.

Vivienne, being an amateur photographer, was in her element and went snap happy crazy, and proceeded in showing them to Bob.

"They are lovely pictures," Bob said, "some of which will, no doubt, end up on Facebook on your story page," he continued.

She replied, "You know me so well!"

At lunchtime they found a quiet spot under a shaded tree, where they sat and ate their cheese and cucumber sandwich, drank cups of tea Vivienne had prepared earlier, and rested. After lunch they walked some more. Later in the afternoon they had some refreshment of orangeade and a few snacks.

They packed up, and left the grounds at five-thirty p.m., and headed for the car, and arrived home in time for the six o'clock news.

"Oh!" Vivienne exclaimed. "From the news headlines it would appear there are soon to be vaccines for the virus but scientists are still doing tests."

Bob was in the kitchen making tea. He said it would be good if they developed one that worked. "How much longer can we go on like this in Lockdown?" he said.

"From what they've said on the news," said Vivienne, "the vaccines are in their early stages and are now being tested."

As the evening went on, most of the conversation surrounded the vaccines, and when they would be rolled out; and who, in their opinion, should be first to get the vaccine. They thought the most vulnerable should be first and the NHS staff who had to work with and care for patients with the disease.

Bob and Vivienne were fairly healthy, and talked about whether either of them would take the vaccine.

Vivienne said, “I think if one is reasonably healthy and showing no symptoms, they may abstain from taking the vaccine; but then,” she said, “from what is being said, one could be asymptomatic; for example, people who are infected with the virus but never develop symptoms. This virus is so complex.”

Bob, the accountant, with his practical head, said for the healthy individuals he thought the vaccine would be a personal choice on whether people take it not. Unless, it became mandatory, that it had to be taken before one returned to a country.

Vivienne said, “But the word healthy is debateable in this case. Are you healthy if you have the virus and show no symptoms of it?”

“Asymptomatic,” Bob replied, “this is where it gets a bit tricky.”

Vivienne said, “Bob do you have garden work planned for tomorrow?”

He replied, “Nothing, that can’t wait.”

“That’s good,” she said. “Tomorrow, for an hour, it might be an idea to catch up on our French; one of the things on our list to do during lockdown.”

“That should be fun,” Bob said. Vivienne was not sure how to take that.

CHAPTER 39

- They met on the Train from Paris to London
- Ils se sont rencontrés dans le train de Paris à Londres

Hello, my name is Juliet. I am eighteen years old. I live in London. What is your name? I am Jonas. I am twenty years old. I live in Paris, France. Juliet: Do you speak English? Jonas: I speak a little English. My first language is French. Juliet: I speak a little French. My first language is English, but my parents have a holiday home near Poitiers in France. Jonas: I can help you with you French speaking You can help me with English? Very good, thank you.	Bonjour, je m'appelle Juliette. J'ai dix-huit ans. J'habite à Londres. Comment tu t'appelles? Je suis Jonas. J'ai vingt ans. Je vis à Paris, France. Juliet: Parlez-vous Anglais ? Jonas: Je parle un peu Anglais. Ma première langue est le Français Juliette: Je parle un peu Français. Ma première langue est l'Anglais, mais mes parents ont une maison de vacances près de Poitiers en France Jonas: Je peux vous aider avec vous Français. Et vous pouvez m'aider avec mon Anglais? Très bien, merci.

Bob and Vivienne did not realise how poor their French speaking was, and the many words they had forgotten. So, they agreed to set aside one hour each day practising French.

Bob et Vivienne n'ont pas réalisé à quel point leur francophone était pauvre et les nombreux mots qu'ils ont oubliés. Ils ont donc convenu de réserver une heure par jour à pratiquer le français.

With revision done for today; Vivienne made lunch of tomato soup and buttered bread rolls, after which they decided to go for a walk as it was a bright day.

Avec la révision faite pour aujourd'hui. Vivienne a fait le déjeuner de soupe aux tomates et de petits pains beurrés. Après quoi, ils ont décidé de se promener car c'était une journée ensoleillée.

CHAPTER 40

It was a pleasant walk along the River Thames and on to Kingston. Bob and Vivienne saw regular walkers with familiar faces, who would nod and smile as they went by; keeping the two-metre distance.

The many cyclists whizzed by close to the walkers at excessive speed; and one could be confused that one was at the Tour de France.

Scrummy mummies jogged along with baby in tow; many walkers and runners, young and old alike.

At Cranbury Park, personal trainers kept themselves busied with one-to-one workout routines, while in other areas of the park, families picnicked, and played with their children and exercised their dogs. Boys played football, whilst others were on their bikes, spinning the wheels and doing tricks; Teenagers and others had their smartphones glued to their ears or were focused reading what was on-screen.

Men and young lads sat on the riverbanks with fishing lines dangling in the Thames for hours in hope of a catch. Picturesque boats with comical names were moored along the river.

The Thames was calm with red canoes rowing to-and-fro, and in the distance, proudly, stood Kingston Bridge, arched over the River Thames.

On the way back the sunset turned bright orange with reflection on the water, and Vivienne captured it on her smartphone, as with many other pictures. A little later on daylight dimmed; and the Thames became alive; with the sparkling lights along the river that made for magical scenery. This clearly showed the lock at its best, and the elevated restaurant on the waterfront.

CHAPTER 41

Being the last gardening day for Bob until spring, he was pretty quick out of the kitchen this morning as there was a lot to be done. In his wellington boots and with hat on head, he pulled up his gloves. The air was crisp and cold and he thought to himself, there was a lot to be done; and the sooner he got started the better. He got his tools from the shed and his large drum with lid for burning; his long garden rake, his wheelbarrow; garden spade and a box of matches in his pocket; and his large water butt at the bottom of the garden.

But before long, he could see Vivienne coming down the garden path in a thick red jumper and black leggings, a pink knitted hat on her head and wearing a bright pair of orange garden gloves.

"Hello, love," she said to Bob. "I thought I'd come down and give you a hand, with there being so much to do."

Bob said, "That's nice of you, love."

Vivienne said, "A job shared is a job halved. Where would you have me start? I know you normally have a system, so just point me in the direction."

Bob said, "Maybe you would like to rake up the leaves into a pile, and put them in the wheelbarrow."

"Okay," said Vivienne. She then went all around the garden and raked the leaves into piles, while Bob gathered the fallen apples into a heap ready for the wheelbarrow. They worked as a team and got much done. Bob emptied the contents of the wheelbarrow on the compost heap each time it got filled. They were almost halfway through and Vivienne went in and made some tea, returning with a mug each for her and Bob. They sat on the bench and drank the tea; once finished they left the mugs on the bench and went back to finish the work in hand. Vivienne had cleared all the leaves and the garden was looking neat.

Vivienne now finished, she picked up the two emptied mugs from the bench and headed back to the kitchen. She said to Bob, "These winter evenings tend to come in early so try not to be long."

"Okay, dear," he replied.

Bob stacked the unwanted bits from the garden into the large drum; he cut back the dead wood from the shrubs and blackberry bushes. He put the rest of the spoiled apples and leaves that could not hold on the compost heap into the big drum for burning, He also pulled out the hidden weeds behind the rosemary bush, into the rubbish drum. Bob then lit a match to the rubbish in the drum and sat on the garden bench and watched as it burned. As he looked across, he realised that the fence was in need of repair so he went to the shed and got a hammer and some nails and in no time the fence was as good as new again.

Bob returned to the garden bench again and sat down looking at the garden rubbish as it burned, and he drifted off, deep in thought, and reminisced about the accountancy job he had retired from. He thought how quickly things had changed with lockdown; about the plans he and Viv had made for retirement, all of which had been put on hold. Bob drifted deeper in thought and compared life in general before lockdown and during lockdown, and how confined life had become. When he suddenly realised that the smoke from the drum begun to spread, he quickly put the lid on the drum containing the smoke. Bob sat there for much longer than he had realised; he then decided to put away his tools and shut the shed door.

Thinking out loud, he said, "Now that a vaccine has been found and tested on individuals, I hope it will not be long before things are normal again and lockdown lifted. Let us hope next year is a better year." He picked up the bucket of water from the butt, lifted the lid, and poured the water on the fire and waited until the flames went out and he headed inside.

Vivienne met him at the kitchen door saying, "All done?"

He replied, "Oh yes."

She handed him a mug of tea and said, "All's well that ends well." and shut the door.